Tiara Friends

Scholastic Children's Books
An imprint of Scholastic Ltd
Euston House, 24 Eversholt Street, London, NW1 1DB, UK
Registered office: Westfield Road, Southam, Warwickshire, CV47 0RA

First published in the UK by Scholastic Ltd, 2016

Trade ISBN 978 1407 17430 3
Book Club ISBN 978 1407 17078 7

A CIP catalogue record for this book
is available from the British Library.

Printed by CPI Group (UK) Ltd, Croydon, CR0 4YY

Papers used by Scholastic Children's Books are made
from wood grown in sustainable forests.

1 3 5 7 9 10 8 6 4 2

Paula Harrison

Tiara Friends

The Secret of the Silk Dress

SCHOLASTIC

For my mum, who is the best mum in the world!

Chapter One

The Quarrelsome Cousins

Millie and Jess hurried down the back stairs of Peveril Palace. Stopping on the bottom step, Jess peeked down the servants' corridor. "It's all right!" she hissed. "There's no one here." Bounding across the passageway, she opened the door to the stable yard.

"Come on, Jax!" Millie dashed through the door and a golden spaniel with floppy ears scampered after her.

The royal stable yard was empty. Millie smiled, watching Jax bound up and down with his tail wagging. It was a lovely morning and the white walls of Peveril Palace were gleaming in the sunshine.

"I can't wait to go horse riding," said Jess. "I'm so glad we swapped!"

"Me too!" Millie grinned. Jess was her best friend and they looked so much alike that they could have been twins! They both had glossy brown hair with golden tints at the front, long eyelashes and upturned noses. They were the same height and both had hazel eyes (although Jess's were a little darker).

Looking exactly the same was really handy and the girls swapped places all the time! That way they both got to do the things they loved best. This time Jess was going riding while Millie gave Jax a bath. Jess had put on Millie's royal riding clothes and a green velvet cloak. Millie was wearing Jess's maid uniform with a little white apron and mob cap.

No one would have guessed that Jess was really the palace maid while Millie was Princess Amelia, daughter of the king and queen!

"This should do for Jax's bath!" Jess pushed a large wooden tub towards the water pump.

Seeing the tub, Jax whined and scampered away towards the stables.

"Jax!" called Millie. "Oh dear! He really doesn't like baths."

The girls chased the golden spaniel, catching him at the corner of the stables. Jax picked up a muddy blue glove in his mouth and dropped it proudly at Millie's feet.

"That's the glove I lost last week." Millie rubbed Jax's coat. "Good boy!"

"He must have known it was yours," said Jess. "He has such a good sense of smell."

Together the girls took Jax to the tub. Jess crouched down and put her arms round the muddy spaniel. He stared back at her with big brown eyes. "Poor old Jax! You've never liked soap and water, have you?"

"But he looks so golden and fluffy afterwards!" Millie turned on the pump. "I want to give him a good wash while you're riding. If I hurry, I can be done before my cousins start searching for me." She smiled as she watched the water froth and swirl into the tub. A princess wasn't supposed to wash dogs – especially in the middle of the stable yard – but now she was wearing Jess's clothes no one would stop her!

She took a bar of soap from her apron pocket. "Ready, Jax!"

"Woof!" Jax sniffed the soap suspiciously.

A loud whinny came from the stables and Jess's eyes lit up. "I should go!" She held out her little finger to Millie. "I'll find you after I've finished riding, Double Trouble!"

Millie linked her pinkie with Jess's. Double Trouble was their secret name. The two girls had been born in the same month and they'd known each other since they were little. Jess's mother was a dressmaker who made clothes for the royal family.

When Jess was old enough she had come to Peveril Palace to work as a maid, and she and Millie had become best friends. This summer they'd even solved their first mystery together when a thief had stolen the baby prince's diamond crown.

Jess turned to go, her riding cloak flapping.

"Come on, Jax!" Millie lifted the reluctant dog into the tub. "I'm going to get you nice and clean."

"PRINCESS AMELIA!"

The shout made the girls jump. Millie twisted round so fast that her mob cap nearly fell off. She clutched at it desperately.

Millie's aunt, Lady Havering, was standing in the doorway, her nose wrinkling at the smell of the stable yard. She was wearing a cream-coloured dress and a wide hat. Her daughters, Veronica and Alice, stood behind her. They had arrived yesterday and were staying at Peveril Palace for a few days.

Millie's cousins were wearing smart dresses and gold bracelets. With her fair hair and wrinkled nose, Veronica looked like a smaller version of her mother. Alice was shorter and had smooth dark hair that hung just above her shoulders.

At nine years old, she was the same age as Millie and Jess, while Veronica was two years older. Alice stood on tiptoes to try and see over her mother's shoulder but Veronica nudged her out of the way.

Jess, who was halfway across the yard, scurried back to Millie. "What shall we do?" she whispered.

"Amelia! Did you hear me?" Lady Havering looked sternly at Jess.

Millie murmured out of the corner of her mouth, "Say something, Jess! Remember – you're supposed to be me!"

"Oh!" Jess turned red and curtsied to Lady Havering. "No, I'm sorry. I didn't hear what you said at all."

Lady Havering frowned. "Veronica and Alice need new clothes, so your mother is taking us all to a dressmaker in Plumchester. You need to get ready immediately." She eyed Jess's outfit. "There's mud all over your cloak. Honestly, Amelia. No one would believe you were a royal princess!"

Jess opened her mouth and closed it again.

"It was my fault," said Millie, wanting to cover for her friend. "I needed a little help with Jax."

Hearing his name, Jax pulled free and leapt out of the tub. He galloped across the stable yard splashing water everywhere. Lady Havering gave a shriek and retreated indoors with Veronica and Alice. Millie and Jess chased after Jax, trying not to giggle.

Millie and Jess dashed to Millie's bedchamber and swapped clothes before rushing downstairs. They nearly knocked over Mr Steen the butler on the palace steps. Two carriages were waiting on the drive. Each one had glossy red doors with a golden crown painted in the middle.

"You're just in time, Amelia!" Queen Belinda smiled at her daughter. "Jess, we'd love you to come too. It's your parents' shop we're visiting after all. You can both sit in the other carriage with Veronica and Alice."

"Thank you, Your Majesty!" said Jess.

Millie beamed. She loved visiting Buttons and Bows, the dressmaking shop run by Jess's mother and father. There was always something new to look at, like patterned ribbons or scarves made from silk. Once she'd found a whole jar of green buttons shaped like frogs with little black eyes.

She and Jess climbed in and Mr Steen closed the carriage door. The coachman shouted to the horses, and the carriage rumbled down the drive and through the palace's golden gates. The streets of Plumchester were crowded with women in bonnets and men in boots and caps. There were stalls selling everything from turnips to candlestick holders. On the corner, a flower seller held out big bunches of roses to the passers-by.

"I don't know why we couldn't have had dresses made at home." Veronica wrinkled her nose. "This place smells awful."

"But you'll love Buttons and Bows!" cried Millie. "Jess's mother is an amazing dressmaker."

Veronica sighed and fiddled with her gold bracelet.

"I'm glad we're here. There's always so much to see in the city." Alice leaned closer to the window.

"Stop squashing me, Alice!" Veronica pushed her sister away. "You're always doing that."

"Ouch!" squeaked Alice. "I only wanted

to look at that flower stall. You don't have to hit me."

Millie and Jess exchanged looks. Millie had often wished that she and Jess were sisters. She had a brother – Prince Edward – who was only one year old. But Alice and Veronica were always arguing and didn't seem to like being sisters at all.

The carriage rolled to a stop in Bodkin Street in front of Buttons and Bows and everyone climbed out. The scent of freshly baked bread drifted across the street from Mr Bibby's bakery. Next door to Buttons and Bows was Miss Clackton's Pet Emporium. Miss Clackton waved to Millie and Jess through the window. She had a black-and-white kitten draped over each shoulder.

Across the road, Mr Heddon scowled at the girls and closed the door to his ironmonger shop. Millie looked away quickly. Mr Heddon was well known for his grumpy manner but today he seemed even more bad-tempered than usual.

"I hope this shop has some elegant cloth," said Lady Havering sternly. "I don't want my daughters wearing shabby materials."

"It does have good cloth, Mother!" cried Alice. "Look!"

Hanging in the window was a long sheet of golden silk that shimmered in the light. Millie thought it was the most beautiful cloth she'd ever seen.

The shop door swung open and Mrs Woolhead, Jess's mother, stood there beaming. "Welcome to Buttons and Bows, everyone!"

Chapter Two

The Golden Silk

Queen Belinda and Lady Havering went into the dressmaking shop, followed by Millie and her cousins. Jess's mother bustled around, finding chairs for the two ladies. Jess came in last. She was pleased to see the smiles on everyone's faces as they gazed round the bright and cosy room.

The shelves along each wall were stacked with neat bundles of cloth. Underneath the glass counter were colourful cotton reels and hundreds of shiny buttons. A tall, silver-edged mirror stood in the middle of the shop ready for any customers trying on new clothes.

Mrs Woolhead began checking Veronica's height with her tape measure while Lady Havering gave out orders. "The skirt *must* reach her ankles," she said, tapping on the counter with her fingernail. "And the hem *has* to be sewn with the utmost neatness."

Jess fetched dozens of brightly coloured bundles of cloth for Lady Havering to inspect. At last, the lady decided that Veronica should have the gold silk they had seen hanging in the window, while Alice's dress should be made from orange satin. The two girls stood still while Mrs Woolhead carefully cut and pinned the material around them.

Veronica stood before the tall mirror. She smiled at her reflection, preening as she smoothed the shimmering silk.

"But, Mother! Why does Veronica get the gold silk?" cried Alice. "I saw it first!"

"Quiet, Alice. I've made up my mind," said Lady Havering.

"It's a shame there isn't enough for two dresses." Mrs Woolhead gave Alice a kindly smile. "But I'm afraid this is the very last of a roll of silk that came on a ship from the east. We don't expect any more till spring."

Mrs Woolhead agreed to finish sewing the dresses, ready for them to be collected the next day. Lady Havering got out her purse to pay while Queen Belinda examined some red ribbon behind the counter.

Veronica smirked at Alice. "The gold silk looks better on me anyway," she said quietly. "And that orange cloth matches your freckles."

Alice scowled at her sister.

"Why don't we go to Mr Bibby's bakery next," suggested Millie, trying to stop an argument. "His cakes are really delicious!"

"We're going to Emerald Alley next," snapped Lady Havering, who had overheard. "I simply *must* take a look in the jewellers' shops."

"Why don't we leave the girls here in Bodkin Street?" said Queen Belinda. "They can buy a cake while we're gone. We'll only be half an hour." She smiled at the girls as she followed Lady Havering into the carriage.

Jess hung back to help her mother tidy the bundles of cloth. "Has Father gone out?"

"He's buying wool at the market." Her mother put the last bundle back on the shelf and wiped her forehead. "Thank you, sweetheart. Now here's half a penny for you to spend at the bakery."

Jess hugged her mother and hurried out of Buttons and Bows. Millie and her cousins were already inside Mr Bibby's, choosing from mouth-watering rows of cakes. Jess picked a berry cupcake topped with purple icing and gave her halfpenny to round-cheeked Mr Bibby.

Alice pointed to Miss Clackton's Pet Emporium. "Look at that red-and-blue parrot in the window. I'd love to go in there!"

"I wouldn't!" Veronica sniffed. "Parrots are such horrid squawky birds."

Alice glared at Veronica. "I think they're funny."

"Why don't you take Alice to Miss Clackton's," Millie said to Jess. "And I'll stay here with Veronica."

Jess nodded. It seemed a good idea to keep Alice and Veronica apart, but she felt sorry for Millie being stuck with the grumpy Veronica!

The parrot in the window flapped its

bright wings as Jess and Alice opened the door to the Pet Emporium. Sleepy kittens in a basket beside the counter pricked up their ears.

"Morning, girls!" Miss Clackton rushed up to them. Her straggly hair was escaping from a bun and her glasses were slipping down her nose. "Hello, Jess! Who is your friend?"

"This is Alice, Princess Amelia's cousin," explained Jess.

Alice looked as if she wanted to pet the kittens but Miss

Clackton took her arm. "Come, my dear! I'll show you round. I have everything you could possibly want to completely pamper your pet. See – these are combs and ribbons for puppies and little doggie mirrors for them to look at themselves."

Jess tried to imagine Jax, the palace spaniel, dressed up in ribbons and staring at himself in a tiny round mirror. She turned away to hide a giggle.

"And here's the storeroom with all the best food for every pet and decorations to make them gorgeous!" Miss Clackton showed Alice the huge storeroom stacked high with tins and boxes. "And this corridor leads right out into the back yard."

"Can I see the parrot?" asked Alice. "Does he talk?"

"Of course you can!" Returning to the main shop, Miss Clackton carefully opened the bird's cage. "Sometimes he says Henry, which is his name, but that's the only word he knows." She held out her hand. "Come here, Henry!"

The parrot ignored her. Flying out of the cage, he swooped over the counter and woke the kittens with a loud squawk. Then he circled the shop five times before flying down the corridor into the storeroom.

"Henry!" gasped Miss Clackton, pushing up her glasses. "Catch him, Jess!"

Jess dashed into the storeroom and found Henry perched on a tower of doggie-treat boxes. At the end of the corridor, a glimpse of blue sky showed that the back door was open. "Quick, Alice!" Jess called over her shoulder. "We have to shut that door before Henry flies away."

"I'll do it!" Alice ran along the passage.

Jess tiptoed towards Henry, who was

eyeing her beadily. Just as she made a grab for the bird, he squawked, "Henry!" Then he took off, sending doggie-treat boxes cascading to the floor. Jess chased him back into the main shop where Miss Clackton was trying to calm the excited kittens. She and Jess chased Henry round and round. When the parrot settled somewhere, they tried to creep closer. But each time Henry waited until they were almost in reach before launching into the air again.

"This isn't working!" gasped Jess.

"I know what might help." Miss Clackton opened a tin and poured sunflower seeds into her hand. "Look, Henry! Treats!"

The parrot gazed at the seeds suspiciously. At last he landed on Miss Clackton's arm and began pecking at the food.

"Such a naughty parrot!" Miss Clackton stroked his feathers before putting him back in his cage. "Look at the mess you've made."

The shop floor was covered with pet combs and bits of sawdust. Jess began sweeping but she stopped when she saw the queen's carriage draw up outside. "Alice, we have to go," she called.

Alice appeared at the storeroom door, her dark hair tangled. "I've tidied up in here as much as I can."

"Thank you, dear! Do come again." Miss Clackton waved as they left.

Jess took Alice to the waiting carriage and the coachman opened the door. "You go ahead," she told the other girl. "I'll fetch Millie and Veronica."

As she rushed across the street a delivery boy ran into her, nearly knocking her over. The boy's cap fell off. It had a stripy grey pattern and was covered with mud. Jess went to pick it up but the boy grabbed it first.

He ran on without even looking at her, clutching a bulging bag with one arm.

Jess frowned. He should at least have said sorry. Straightening up, she noticed Mr Heddon in the ironmonger shop, glaring at her through the window. She wondered why he looked so cross.

"Jess!" Her mother dashed out of Buttons and Bows. "You didn't take the dress, did you?"

Jess stared at her. "What dress?"

"The gold silk dress that I'm making for Lady Havering," said her mother.

"What do you mean?" A feeling of dread slid down Jess's insides.

"I only went upstairs to fetch another needle." Mrs Woolhead crumpled her apron in her hands. "But when I came down the dress was gone."

Chapter Three
The Empty Hanger

Jess gazed at her mother, wide-eyed. "The dress has gone? But where?"

"I don't know." Mrs Woolhead looked pale. "I've searched all around the shop. Then I thought perhaps one of you had collected it."

Jess glanced at Veronica and Millie on the other side of the street. They were talking and pointing to the cakes in the window of Mr Bibby's. Neither of them was carrying the dress. "No, none of us has it."

The door of the queen's carriage swung open and Lady Havering peered out. Jess's mind worked fast. If Lady Havering discovered that the dress was missing she'd cause a terrible scene. They had to find it before anyone realized what was happening.

Jess rushed into Buttons and Bows. Her heart thumped loudly. She had to calm down and think. Where could the dress be?

"I'll look upstairs just in case," said her mother, hurrying to the wooden stairs.

"I'll check down here." Jess opened the drawers behind the counter one by one. She looked under balls of wool and folded cloth. She checked every roll of material on the shelves. There was no sign of the gold silk dress anywhere.

Alice's orange satin dress hung beside the counter. Next to it was an empty hanger where the gold silk dress had been.

"Jess!" Millie burst in, making the bell on the door jingle. "We're all waiting for you. Are you ready to go?"

Jess, who was looking under her mother's sewing table, stumbled to her feet. "Oh, Millie! Something awful has happened!"

"What's the matter?" Millie came inside. "Are you all right?"

"I'm looking for the dress—" Jess broke off as she saw Veronica and Alice crowding in behind Millie.

"What dress?" Veronica noticed the empty hanger. "Where's my gold silk dress? Have you lost it?"

"I'm sure it must be here somewhere," said Jess desperately.

Veronica dashed out of the shop. "Mother,

come quickly!" she called. "My beautiful gold silk dress is GONE!"

Mrs Woolhead came down the steps, her hair ruffled. "It isn't upstairs. Oh dear, I don't understand where it could be."

Just then Lady Havering marched through the door with Veronica and Queen Belinda behind her. "Mrs Woolhead, what on earth is going on? Veronica tells me her gold silk dress is missing."

Mrs Woolhead clasped her hands tightly. "I'm afraid it's true. I really don't know... I only went upstairs for a minute and that's when it disappeared."

Jess frowned. At first she'd thought her mother might have mislaid the dress, but the way it had vanished seemed suspicious. She exchanged glances with Millie. "We should check the storeroom," she said quickly. "We haven't looked in there."

"I'll help you." Millie rushed after her.

Jess lit a lamp and closed the storeroom door. Racks of dresses filled up most of the space. In the corner was a hat stand which looked like an odd sort of tree.

"Jess," whispered Millie. "Don't you think there's something strange about this? Your mother would never have lost that dress – she's much too careful – and if it slipped off its hanger we'd have found it by now."

"I think someone's taken it," replied Jess.

Millie's eyes widened. "But how? Surely someone would have seen them."

The handle turned and Veronica stood in the doorway. "Why are you still in here? Did you find my dress?"

Millie shook her head. "No, it's not in here. Sorry!"

Lady Havering's raised voice made them all jump. "I can't *quite* believe what I'm hearing! You're saying you have no idea where it is?"

Jess hurried out of the storeroom. Lady Havering's face was flushed and her toffee-coloured hat perched crookedly on her head.

Queen Belinda spoke calmly. "This isn't helping, Lucinda. We should go now – give Mrs Woolhead a chance to look again without so many people in the shop."

"The point is," Lady Havering's voice grew sharper, "this woman took my money *before* she lost the silk!"

Jess's cheeks burned. She was about to tell Lady Havering exactly how mean she was being, but Millie put a hand on her arm.

"I assure you I won't stop looking until I find it," said Mrs Woolhead.

Lady Havering marched out of the shop, making the bell jangle. Veronica and Alice followed their mother without a word.

Queen Belinda pressed Mrs Woolhead's hand. "I'm so sorry about this commotion! My sister will calm down, I'm sure." She turned to Millie and Jess. "We must go, girls. Leaving the royal carriages in the street has started to draw a crowd. I really don't want any more fuss!"

Jess wanted to stay and help her mother, but she didn't like to disobey the queen. People were gathering outside the shop and looking in curiously. Jess thought Lady Havering's loud voice had probably drawn them as much as the royal carriages.

"You go, my dear," her mother told her. "You're needed at the palace."

"Goodbye." Jess hugged her mother.

Millie took Jess's arm and the girls left Buttons and Bows. They climbed into the carriage and sat down opposite Millie's cousins. Veronica's mouth was turned down sulkily. Alice was staring out of the window.

The coachman shook the reins and the horses walked on. As the carriage rolled down the street, Jess saw Mr Heddon watching from the doorway of the ironmonger's and shaking his head.

Chapter Four
Seeing Double

Millie watched the streets of Plumchester sweep past the window. Her mind was whirling faster than the carriage wheels. How could someone take a gold silk dress from Buttons and Bows like that? It was obvious that her aunt was blaming Jess's mother, which seemed very unfair.

"It's not right!" Veronica burst out. "I stood still for ages being measured and now I don't have a dress at all."

"You'll still get a dress," said Alice, turning away from the window. "It'll just be a different one."

"I'm not wearing that horrible orange colour like you," said Veronica, making Alice flush. "Why didn't anyone stop that delivery boy on the street? I bet he was the thief. He looked suspicious *and* he had something in his bag."

"That doesn't mean he took the dress," Millie put in. "It could have been anybody." She exchanged looks with Jess. She was sure her friend was thinking the same thing: they had to find out what had happened; not for Veronica, who probably had lots of dresses, but for Jess's mum, who must be really worried.

The girls fell silent as the carriage rumbled through the palace gates and up the long drive. When they arrived, Lady Havering

sent Veronica and Alice to wash their hands and faces.

Millie hurried after Jess, glad to be free of her cousins. "Isn't Veronica awful?" she said, as they turned into the kitchen corridor.

Jess whirled round, her face serious. "I have to get back to Buttons and Bows as soon as I can. Mother will need my help to find that dress."

"We should both help!" Millie pulled Jess into the laundry room and closed the door. A large tub stood in the corner and stacks of neatly folded sheets lay on the shelves. "If someone stole that gold silk we can solve the mystery together just like we did with Edward's crown." She held out her pinkie. "We're Double Trouble!"

Jess linked her little finger with Millie's. "We can go back there and look for clues!"

"Exactly!" Millie's eyes gleamed. "Someone must have seen something important. We should take a pencil and write everything down."

"Good idea! There were quite a few people in Bodkin Street this morning. There was the coachman and Mr Heddon in the ironmonger's. He always seems to be looking out of his window."

"Hold on!" said Millie excitedly. "I'll fetch some paper and write this down." She wrenched the door open to find Mr Steen the butler standing on the other side.

Mr Steen bowed, bending his long thin body awkwardly. "I hope I'm not interrupting, Princess Amelia, but I require Jess for several urgent tasks." He turned to Jess. "All the royal chambers must be swept and every bed made perfectly. Then the silverware in the banquet hall needs polishing."

"Yes, sir," said Jess.

"Connie has gone to fetch some flour and milk from the market so you must finish the cleaning on your own. Hurry up now!" Mr Steen fixed Jess with a stern look before marching away.

Jess sighed. "Now I'll never get back to Buttons and Bows. Those jobs will take me the rest of the day."

Millie beamed. "Not if there are two Jesses instead of one! I'll start on the polishing while you sweep. I'll wear your spare maid uniform and no one will know it's really me!"

Jess bit her lip. "I guess we'd finish quicker."

"It'll be fun – much better than listening to Veronica and Alice arguing all morning." Millie pulled a face which made Jess laugh.

Hurrying to Jess's chamber, Millie changed into the maid clothes and hid her royal dress in Jess's wardrobe. Lastly she tucked her hair inside a white mob cap and looked in the little square mirror that hung on the wall.

There was a knock at the door and Jess

came in. Millie smiled at her friend. "Now we look like twins again!"

The cuckoo clock in the palace entrance hall chimed eleven. "I'll meet you back here in two hours." Jess grabbed a broom before hurrying towards the stairs. "Then we can start writing down those clues."

"The last one back is a goose's tail!" Millie called after her.

Polishing the silverware in the banquet hall took longer than Millie expected. There were so many silver cups, plates and candlesticks, and they all needed a lot of cleaning. Millie frowned as she rubbed another dish. She had to make it shine until she could see her own face, otherwise Mr Steen would make her start all over again.

The cuckoo clock in the palace hallway chimed again. Had the first hour gone already? When the polishing was done, she ran upstairs to look for Jess. Veronica and Alice passed her in the corridor, but she pulled her cap down low and they hardly looked at her.

There was no sign of Jess in the royal bedchambers. Millie collected some paper and a pencil from her own chamber and hid them in her apron pocket. Then she climbed the steps to the top floor. Mr Larum, her tutor, was sitting at his desk in the schoolroom writing down mathematical sums.

"Hello, Mr Larum," Millie said cheerfully. "Have you seen … oh!" She stopped as she saw Jess sweeping on the opposite side of the room.

"Hmm? What was that?" said Mr Larum.

Millie rushed out just as the tutor lifted his head. Dodging round the corner, she leaned against the wall by the stairs. Her heart was pounding.

"Jess?" Mr Larum sounded puzzled. "Did you say something just now?"

"I said, have you seen … the weather?" said Jess. "It's lovely and sunny!"

Mr Larum coughed. "The funny thing is … for a moment I'm sure I saw two of you – one over here and one over there. I must be seeing double!"

Millie put her hand over her mouth and peeked round the door. Her tutor had taken off his spectacles. "Oh dear!" he said, rubbing his eyes. "Perhaps I've been working for too long. I'd better have a lie down!"

"Take care, Mr Larum," said Jess, hurrying out. "I hope you feel better."

"That was close!" giggled Millie, as the girls escaped down the stairs.

"That was *really* close! Poor Mr Larum!" Jess grinned. "I've finished all my chores."

"Me too! And I've got this." Millie waved the paper at her friend. "Shall we take Jax with us?" She turned to Jax who was sleeping on his rug outside the laundry room. "Ready for a walk, Jax?" The spaniel jumped up, barking loudly. Millie patted his golden fur and gathered up his lead.

There were footsteps on the stairs.

"That could be Mr Steen!" hissed Jess.

Millie put a finger to her lips and the girls crept to the back door. The stable yard was busy with horses and carriages. Millie glanced nervously behind her but she didn't dare to run in case it looked suspicious.

At last they turned the corner by the stables. Now they were far away from palace windows and watching eyes. The hill stretched down to the lake and the water glistened in the bright sunshine.

Millie noticed how quiet Jess was. "Are you thinking about Veronica's dress?"

"I'm trying to remember if there was anyone acting suspiciously in Bodkin Street," Jess told her. "Whoever it was they'll never guess that we're the ones looking for them." She started running down the slope. "Come on, I'll race you!"

"Wait for me!" called Millie, clutching her mob cap to stop it falling off.

The girls ran down the hill and Jax chased after them, barking with excitement.

Chapter Five

Back to Bodkin Street

When they reached the lake, Jess held on to Jax's lead tightly. The golden spaniel loved going for a swim and there was no time for that today. They crossed the wooden bridge. The wind whipped up little waves on the lake's surface. Climbing the slope on the other side, they stopped at a line of thick bushes.

Jess peered through the undergrowth.

Behind the bushes were the black iron railings that surrounded the palace grounds. Jess had discovered a loose railing one day when Jax got stuck in the bushes. She and Millie had been using it as a secret way to leave the palace ever since.

She bit her lip. She wished Mr Steen hadn't kept her back with that list of chores. Her mother must be so worried about the missing dress.

"Over here!" Millie pointed to a crooked railing. "I'm sure that's the right one."

Jess plunged into the bushes, ignoring the scratches on her arms and ankles. She pushed the railing and it swung aside with a rusty creak. Holding it steady, she let Millie and Jax go past before squeezing through herself.

On the other side was a quiet lane with a row of neat houses. Jess and Millie hurried up the street and round the corner, passing

Halfpenny Square with its busy shops and market stalls. A few minutes later they turned into Bodkin Street.

Jess's heart sank when she saw a sign in the window of Buttons and Bows. "*We are closed for the rest of the day*," she read. "*Please come back tomorrow.*"

"But the shop's always open!" cried Millie. "Why would your mother and father close it? Do you think they're all right?"

"I don't know." Jess pushed the door handle but found the door was locked. Her stomach lurched. Her parents had never locked the door in the daytime before. Cupping her hands to the glass, she peered through the window. It was dark inside.

Millie knocked on the door but there was no answer.

"Maybe Mr Bibby knows where my parents went." Jess dashed across the street to the bakery. "Mr Bibby, did you see my mother before she left? The shop's all locked up."

"She left this for you." Mr Bibby dropped a silver key into Jess's hand. "She seemed in a bit of a hurry."

"Thank you!" Jess wanted to ask whether her mother had left a message, but the bakery was full of people and Mr Bibby turned away to serve the next customer. Hurrying back to Buttons and Bows, Jess unlocked the door and the girls stepped inside.

Alice's orange satin dress was still hanging behind the counter. Millie spotted a scribbled note beside the till. "There's a message!" She read it out. "*Dear Jess, I've gone to the harbour to find out if any ships are bringing more gold silk from the east. Father is still at the wool market. Please don't worry, love, Mother.*"

Jess sighed. "I don't think she'll have any

luck. The captain of the last ship said there would be no more gold silk arriving till next spring."

"I guess she felt she had to try." Millie wrinkled her brow. "It sounds like she's given up on finding the dress though."

"Let's look again just in case we missed something before." Jess patted Jax who had laid down on the floor. "Wait here, Jax. Good boy!"

Together Millie and Jess opened every drawer in the shop. They climbed on chairs to search all the high shelves. They checked every part of the store cupboard and went up the stairs to search the rooms at the top of the house. They even went out into the yard at the back and hunted around the wooden seat and the pots of lavender.

"Yoo hoo!" Miss Clackton came through a gate from the yard next door. The back yard of the Pet Emporium was only separated from the dress shop's by a wooden fence. "Hello, Jess! Have you brought a friend from the palace?"

"Yes, this is M—" Jess broke off as Millie nudged her. She'd almost forgotten her friend was wearing maid clothes. "Um ... this is Maggie."

"Pleased to meet you!" Miss Clackton beamed. "Isn't that amazing! You look almost like twins."

"Hello!" Millie smiled and bobbed a curtsy.

"Miss Clackton, did you see my mother go out? How long ago did she set off?" asked Jess.

"Well, let me see." Miss Clackton pushed her glasses on more firmly. "I think she left not long ago – ten minutes perhaps. She looked as if she was in an awful hurry. Is everything all right?"

"A gold silk dress got taken from the shop this morning," explained Millie.

Miss Clackton put a hand to her mouth. "Oh, how awful!"

"Did you see anything?" said Jess urgently. "Maybe someone who looked suspicious?"

"Goodness!" Miss Clackton blinked rapidly. "I only saw Queen Belinda and Princess Amelia with their guests. After that I don't know. You remember how my parrot, Henry, made all that mess, don't you, Jess? I've been busy tidying up all day. Such a naughty bird!"

Jess swallowed her disappointment. "Thanks, Miss Clackton! We'd better get back to our search."

"Good luck, my dears! I'll look out for anyone acting strangely. You can't be too careful these days!" Miss Clackton gave them a little wave before closing the gate.

"We have to discover who took the dress," Jess told Millie as they went back inside. "It's the only way we'll get it back."

"Let's work out some clues." Millie whipped the paper and pencil out of her apron pocket. She put the paper on the counter and smoothed out the creases. "The gold silk dress was taken early in the morning. We had all left the shop and gone to Mr Bibby's bakery to buy cakes. . ."

"Yes, whoever it was only had about a quarter of an hour between all of us leaving the shop and my mother discovering that the dress was missing," Jess put in.

"And they had to come in here whilst your mother was upstairs fetching something, otherwise they'd have been spotted." Millie chewed on the end of the pencil, before writing *quarter of an hour.* "Actually, that's a bit scary! Do you think the thief was watching the shop the whole time and waiting for the right moment?"

Jess shivered. "But why just take one dress? Why not take lots of cloth, sell it and get lots of money?"

"The gold silk was the most expensive thing in the shop," Millie pointed out. "And it's very rare." She scribbled down *gold silk* and *rare*.

"I suppose so. But who would be horrible enough to walk in and take it?"

"Hmm." Millie frowned and wrote *WHO?* in capital letters before underlining it five times.

"That delivery boy that bumped into me was in an awful hurry. There were other people in the street too. It had to be one of them." Jess paced up and down. She tried to picture the people who had been in Bodkin Street that morning. It was hard to remember them all.

"I wish I'd been looking around more carefully. All I remember is Veronica and Alice arguing in the bakery."

"I bet I know someone that was looking.

He's probably watching the street right now." Jess hurried to the shop window.

"Who?" Millie's eyes widened.

Jess pointed to the ironmonger's shop, where a scowling face peered out from behind the curtains. "Look over there! If anyone saw what happened, it's Mr Heddon."

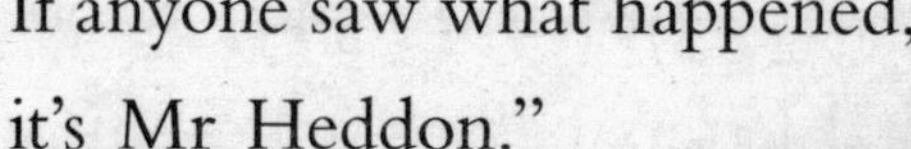

Chapter Six

The Mystery in the Cupboard

"You're right!" Millie gazed across the street. "Mr Heddon's always staring out of the window. He might have seen the thief walk in!"

"I'm going to ask him." Jess dashed outside.

"Jess – wait!" called Millie. "What if he doesn't want to talk to us? He's ever so grumpy."

But Jess was already halfway across the

street. Millie grabbed her pencil and the paper and caught up just as Jess pushed open the door to the ironmonger's. The shop had a musty smell that made Millie want to sneeze. Rows of dull grey kettles and irons stood on the shelves. The floor was strewn with boxes filled with nails, door handles and brass door knockers.

Millie tripped over a wooden crate full of large rusty keys and had to grab hold of a shelf to steady herself. The shelf wobbled and a kettle crashed to the floor.

"What on earth are you DOING?" Mr Heddon rose from his stool behind the counter. He had a tall but slightly stooping frame and grey eyebrows that jutted out above his dark eyes.

"I'm sorry! It was an accident." Millie picked the kettle up quickly and put it back on the shelf.

"Be more careful next time," grumbled Mr Heddon. "What do you want anyway?"

"I'm Jess. I'm the daughter of Mr and Mrs Woolhead who own the dressmaking shop," began Jess. "I just need to ask you some questions."

"I know who you are." The old man pulled his jacket tighter as he sat down again. "But this is an ironmonger's. I sell nails and doorknobs, not answers to questions."

"It won't take long. We promise!" said Millie.

Jess's cheeks flushed. She told Mr Heddon how the dress had gone missing from Buttons and Bows that morning and how important and expensive it was.

"So if you were watching the street this morning you might have seen who went in and took it," finished Millie. "Did you see anyone? Could you describe them?"

Jess clasped her hands together hopefully. Millie got her pencil ready to write down the description.

"No one went in," Mr Heddon told them.

Millie and Jess exchanged looks. "But there must have been *somebody*," said Millie, stepping closer. "If you think really hard maybe you'll remember—"

Mr Heddon shut a door under the counter and it closed with a snap. Millie blinked. Had there been a glint of gold inside that cupboard?

"I was watching the street all morning. No one went through that door except the queen and her guests!" barked Mr Heddon. "Now, go away and stop wasting my time!"

"Sorry!" Millie gulped and the girls ran outside.

"He's such a grouch!" cried Jess, as soon as they were safely across the street. "It can't be right that no one went into the shop except us. Dresses don't just vanish!"

"What if he's not telling the truth?" Millie's eyes went very round. "He was in a big hurry to close that cupboard under his counter just now. What if the dress is in there?"

Jess frowned. "I don't understand why he'd take it though."

"Maybe he plans to sell it." Millie went into Buttons and Bows. "I'm going to look inside that cupboard and find out!"

Jax got to his feet, his tail wagging, and Jess rubbed his golden coat. "You'll never get back into that place. Mr Heddon was really cross."

Millie beamed. "I can go back in disguise!" She was about to explain her plan when she caught sight of a face at the window. Her heart jumped. "Jess, look!

Isn't that the same boy who knocked you over this morning?"

Jess swung round. "What's he doing here?"

The boy with the stripy grey cap was leaning close to the window to look in, his nose pressed against the glass. He stepped

back when he met Millie's stare. Pulling his bag over his shoulder, he ran off down the street.

"Go after him!" Millie urged Jess. "I'll stay here and search Mr Heddon's place."

"Meet you back at the palace!" Jess flung herself out of the door with Jax galloping at her heels.

Millie went to the storeroom and searched the racks of clothes. She wondered for a moment if it was right to borrow something without asking Mrs Woolhead. It was fine as long as it helped them find the missing dress, she decided. She would put it straight back afterwards.

Laying her maid uniform aside, she picked out a pair of breeches and a plain tunic. Then she found a brown cloth cap in a box. Putting it on, she went to check her reflection in the tall mirror. She looked almost like a boy! The shoes weren't right though. She took off her mauve satin shoes. They had been hidden under the maid uniform but she couldn't wear them with boys' breeches!

After searching through several crates at the back of the store room, she found a pair of boys' boots. They were a bit big and they slipped when she walked, but they would have to do.

Millie crept to the window. She'd have to wait until Mr Heddon was busy with a customer. She fixed her eyes on the ironmonger's shop. At last an old lady with a large basket went inside. Millie slipped out of the door of Buttons and Bows and crossed the street.

Mr Heddon was at the far end of his shop, talking to the lady with the basket. Millie tiptoed in, careful not to let the door bang. Crouching down, she crawled to the counter and reached for the cupboard door.

Her heart thumped as she pulled it open.

Inside was a huge bag of peppermints in shiny, gold wrappers. Millie sighed. She'd been so sure that Mr Heddon was hiding something, but perhaps he just didn't like sharing his sweets. Closing the cupboard again, she tiptoed to the door.

"Hey, boy!" called Mr Heddon. "I didn't see you come in. What are you up to?"

Millie pulled her cap over her eyes. "Nothing, sir. Just looking around." She stuck her hands in her pockets.

"If you want to buy something, come over here and tell me what you're looking for," said Mr Heddon.

"Sorry, I've got to go!" squeaked Millie and she dashed out of the shop before he could catch her.

Chapter Seven
Alfie

Jess raced down Bodkin Street with Jax scampering behind her. The delivery boy sped up, his bag bouncing against his side.

"Come back!" shouted Jess.

The boy glanced at her and quickened his pace again. Turning into a cobbled lane, he dodged round a woman with a basket of apples before running on.

Jess pumped her arms as hard as she could. She was a fast runner but this boy was even faster. She wouldn't let him escape. He must know something about the missing dress. Why else would he be trying to get away?

The boy dashed into a narrow alley. Jess's legs began to feel like jelly and her breath burned in her chest. Jax ran beside her, his tongue hanging out.

The boy turned another corner. Lines of washing were strung across the narrow space between the houses. The boy ducked under a row of sheets and vanished. Jess bent over, gasping for breath. The boy must be trying to lose her in the twisted alleyways but she knew this place too well to get lost. She also knew this alley was a dead end. The boy was trapped!

Jax barked and wagged his tail as if it was all an exciting game. The boy reappeared, pushing his way between the sheets. He stopped in front of Jess, his face sulky. "What do you want?"

"Why are you running away?" Jess glared back.

"None of your business!" The boy had a streak of soot across his forehead.

Jess noticed he kept a tight hold of his leather satchel. "What's in there?" She pointed to it.

"That's none of your business either."

Jess studied his scowling face. She might as well ask him straight out. "A silk dress went missing from Buttons and Bows yesterday morning. Did you take it?"

The boy's mouth dropped open. "That's why you're chasing me? Why would I take a *dress*? I'm not gonna wear it, am I?"

Jess hesitated. The boy looked so surprised. "Well you were there at the time. You bumped into me, remember? Then you ran away like you did just now."

"I'm always running! I've got deliveries to make and Mr Weller gives me a clip round the ear if I'm late." He rubbed his boot heel against the cobbles. "And I was afraid you'd think badly of me for staring into a ladies clothes shop just now."

"Oh!" Jess could see he felt awkward about it. "So why did you look in?"

"I've never seen the shop all closed up like that before. I wondered if Mrs Woolhead was all right." He leaned down to pat Jax who was sniffing his boot. "She's a nice lady! She gives me a currant bun when I bring her a parcel."

Jess smiled. "She's my mother, but I don't stay in Bodkin Street all the time because I work at the palace. I'm Jess."

"Pleased to meet yer! I'm Alfie." The boy patted his bag. "I'd better go – got one more delivery to make."

"Hey, wait!" said Jess. "Yesterday, before you bumped into me, did you see anyone go into Buttons and Bows? We were only away from the shop for a few minutes and that's when the dress was stolen."

"Let's see . . . I went to give a letter to the butcher. Then I came back and ran into you." Alfie screwed his face up, thinking. "I didn't see anybody walk in but there was someone already inside the first time I went by."

"Who was it? What did they look like?"

Alfie shook his head. "I don't remember."

Jess's heart sank. "Did you see anything?"

"Just someone standing in front of a mirror holding a dress. Then I ran on cos I knew I was late."

"Was it a gold dress?"

"Um, maybe." Alfie frowned. "I think it was shiny. Sorry I haven't been much help. I'll keep an eye out for the frock, I promise!"

"Thanks!" said Jess. "If you think of anything else send a message to me at the palace."

"All right then, palace girl!" Alfie grinned, calling over his shoulder as he left. "Just imagine if you could dress up like them royal folks!"

Jess crouched down to rub Jax's coat. "If only he knew that I already do!"

Jess's legs began to ache as she hurried through the streets of Plumchester. Jax seemed tired too. Jess longed to go back to Bodkin Street to see if her mother had returned but she knew there wasn't time. Mr Steen had probably thought of another long list of chores for her and Cook would need help preparing dinner.

She moved the loose railing and slipped back through the palace fence. Heavy clouds had drifted across the sky and the lake looked grey and cold. Jess tried to ignore the worried feeling inside her but it wouldn't go away. It was obvious that Alfie had nothing to do with the dress going missing. So who could it have been?

Cook Walsh fussed over her as soon as she reached the kitchen. "You shouldn't skip lunch, you know. It won't do you any good." She set down a bowlful of soup and a thick piece of buttered bread in front of Jess.

"Thank you!" Jess took a spoonful of the delicious hot tomato soup. "I've been so busy I didn't realize how hungry I was."

Cook wiped her hands on her apron. "What's made you so flustered? I've hardly seen you all day."

"Something awful happened." Jess told her about the missing dress and all their efforts to find it.

Cook listened thoughtfully. "What a shame! And the silk dress was meant to be Alice's, was it? No wonder she didn't eat much of the lunch I made them."

"No, the dress was Veronica's," said Jess. "I know she was disappointed but she must have lots of dresses."

"You're fretting about your mother and the shop, aren't you?" Cook patted her shoulder. "Don't you worry! The truth will come out in the end."

Jess took her bowl and plate to the big stone basin to wash them up. She hoped Cook was right, but she didn't feel they were any closer to the truth. Maybe Millie had discovered something. Jess crossed her fingers, hoping that a clue had appeared while she was chasing Alfie.

They had to find the silk dress soon. Lady Havering was so cross she might return to Buttons and Bows and make another fuss. It would be awful if customers stopped coming into the shop, believing the missing dress was all her mother's fault.

Chapter Eight

The Strangest Clue

Millie and Jess didn't get a chance to talk in secret right away. The queen asked Millie to entertain her cousins with board games after dinner. They played Fox and Geese which went well until Alice beat her sister and then Veronica refused to play any more.

Queen Belinda and Lady Havering were talking by the fire. King James was bouncing Prince Edward on his knee. At last, Millie's little brother began to yawn and the king took him upstairs to bed.

Millie's head ached from listening to her cousins argue and she was glad to go upstairs for bedtime. Setting down a lamp on her bedside table, she took off her emerald tiara and brushed her hair.

The curtains shook. "Millie! I'm over here." Jess was sitting on the window seat with her legs tucked up and her arms around her knees.

"Jess! I'm so glad we can talk at last." Millie sank on to the seat beside her friend. "Did you catch the delivery boy?"

"Yes, he's called Alfie," Jess told her. "But he wasn't the one that took the dress. Did you find anything in that cupboard in Mr Heddon's shop?"

"Only peppermints." Millie pulled a face.

"Then we're getting nowhere!" cried

Jess. "If we don't find the dress soon, Lady Havering will want her money back. What if my parents run out of pennies? They'll have to close the shop."

Millie bit her lip. "There *has* to be an answer to all of this. Dresses don't just vanish! I'm going to look at the clues again." She went to her stocking drawer where she'd hidden the paper and pencil. As she returned to the window seat, there was a creaking sound outside the door.

Millie flapped a hand at Jess. That was probably her mother who'd want to know why she wasn't in bed yet. Jess pulled the curtains across, hiding the window seat completely.

There was another creak. Then silence.

Millie tiptoed to the door and peeped into the passageway. There was no one there. Perhaps she'd imagined the noise. Going back to the window seat, she smoothed the paper on her knee. "This is what we've found out so far. The dress was taken this morning just after we left Buttons and Bows, but Mr Heddon told us he didn't see anyone going in or out of the shop."

"That's the strangest clue!" said Jess. "How can someone have got in without being seen? Mr Heddon said he was watching the street the whole time."

Millie shook her head. "Maybe he's wrong about that. Our other clue was the delivery boy but we can rule him out now you've said it wasn't him—"

"He did see someone in the shop though," Jess put in.

Millie's eyes lit up. "Really? Who was it?"

"He's not sure. He couldn't see them very well, but he said they were standing in front of the mirror, holding a dress."

Millie scribbled on the paper. *Standing in front of mirror holding dress.* "So we're looking for someone who got inside without anyone noticing and stood in front of the mirror with the dress." She underlined the word *mirror.* "It's a strange thing for a thief to do. It almost sounds as if they wanted to try the dress on."

"Maybe that's it!" Jess jumped up. "We've been thinking that the thief stole the dress for money, but perhaps they just wanted to wear it."

"We're looking for a girl then – maybe one who hasn't got any nice clothes."

"Tomorrow we can go back to Bodkin Street and look for girls who live nearby." Jess spun round. "Find the girl – find the dress!"

There was a knock at the door. Jess broke off mid-spin and dropped to the floor behind the bed.

"Millie, you should be asleep by now," the queen called. "I hope you're ready for bed."

"Nearly ready," Millie called back, trying not to giggle at Jess's strange move. "Goodnight, Mother."

After the queen's footsteps faded, Jess took the paper and wrote: *Find the girl that liked the dress.* "That's what we'll do tomorrow." She grinned at Millie.

Millie grabbed Jess's arm and spun them both round. "Then Veronica will have her dress back and everything will be all right again!"

When Millie came down to breakfast the next morning, rain was pattering against the palace windows. Veronica and Alice were both eating their breakfast in silence. Millie wondered whether they'd had another argument. Queen Belinda was trying to stop little Edward throwing his toast on the floor.

"I simply cannot go out in weather like this," Lady Havering told the queen. "We'll have to delay any further shopping. Perhaps Veronica and Alice can join Amelia for one of her dancing lessons?"

Millie's heart sank. She didn't like dancing

lessons very much. She always seemed to use the wrong foot and end up in a tangle. "I don't have a dancing teacher at the moment," she told her aunt.

"Then *I* shall instruct you all." Lady Havering rose from the breakfast table and performed a stiff plié, bending her knees and straightening them. "I was the delight of my dancing mistress when I was your age!"

Millie glanced at Jess, who was placing a jug of milk on the table. If she was stuck in Lady Havering's dance lesson, how could she help her friend investigate the missing dress?

Jess came to Millie's bedchamber after breakfast. "I'm going back to Buttons and Bows. A message came from my mother this morning. She didn't find any gold silk for sale."

Millie looked at the rain beating against the glass. She went to her wardrobe and took out a thick, black cloak. "Take my winter cloak. It'll keep you dry."

"Thanks, Millie—" Jess broke off and peeked round the door into the hallway.

"What's the matter?" asked Millie.

"It's your aunt! She sounds really cross," said Jess.

Millie came to listen. Lady Havering was standing in the doorway of Alice's bedchamber. "What do you mean, you don't know where it is?" she snapped. "Tell me where you were keeping it."

"It was here in my drawer," said Alice faintly.

Queen Belinda came out of her bedchamber and hurried along the passage. "Is something the matter, Lucinda?"

Lady Havering's cheeks were flushed with

anger. "First Veronica's dress goes missing, and now Alice's ebony jewellery box has been stolen! There's a thief in this palace. That's the only way to explain it!"

Chapter Nine

The Ebony Jewellery Box

Jess exchanged looks with Millie. The palace was protected by guards at the gate. Surely a thief couldn't have got in?

"Oh dear!" Queen Belinda went pale. "It was bad enough when Edward's crown went missing a few weeks ago."

"Aha! So this has happened before." Lady Havering began pacing up and down the corridor. "Maybe you should start by checking everyone's chambers." She glared around, her eyes settling on Jess. "And what about you? Have you seen an ebony jewellery box?"

"No, Lady Havering, I haven't seen it anywhere." Jess's eyes widened.

"You were with us when the silk dress disappeared too,"

said Lady Havering. "Perhaps you wanted a silk dress and some jewels."

Jess swallowed, feeling that everyone was staring at her. How could Lady Havering think she might be the thief? "I haven't done anything wrong!"

Millie took Jess's hand. "Jess would never take Alice's jewellery box. She's my friend and she'd never take anything that wasn't hers."

"Lucinda, I have known Jess since she was little and she's a very dependable girl," said Queen Belinda firmly. "There's no doubt in my mind that she cannot have been involved."

Lady Havering's brow wrinkled. "Well! It all seems very suspicious to me. There's certainly a robber about somewhere."

"Mother, please listen!" cried Alice. "Nobody stole the jewellery box. I . . . um . . . gave it away."

"You did what?" screeched Lady Havering. "There are necklaces in that box worth more than a gold sovereign . . . and your bracelet with the rubies on. Didn't you think about that?"

Alice's head drooped. She twisted her hair ribbon between her fingers.

"My dear Alice," said Queen Belinda, "what on earth made you give your jewellery away?"

"I wanted to make some money," Alice said at last. "So I asked the butler to take the box into Plumchester and sell everything. I think he's already taken it away."

Lady Havering gave a shriek and swayed on her feet.

Veronica came out of her bedchamber. "What's happening?"

"Quick, Alice!" The queen clasped Lady

Havering's arm. "Fetch your mother's fan. Amelia, help me, please."

Millie took hold of Lady Havering's other arm. Her aunt wobbled, her eyes half-closed.

Jess whispered into Millie's ear. "I'll see if I can find Mr Steen and the jewellery box."

Millie nodded and Jess sped away. Reaching the gallery, she ran past the rows of bookshelves. She raced down the stairs two at a time, nearly running into Connie who was sweeping the floor of the entrance hall.

"Connie!" she gasped. "I'm looking for Mr Steen. Has he gone out?"

Connie looked up. Her hair was escaping from the sides of her mob cap. "Running around instead of doing yer chores again? I'm not doing your work as well as my own."

"I know you aren't," replied Jess. "But where's Mr Steen?"

"Are you looking for me?"

Jess jumped. The lanky butler was standing right behind her. He must have come out of a door nearby without making a sound. "Yes, sir! I need to ask you about the jewellery box Alice gave you," she said quickly. "Have you still got it?"

The butler lifted one eyebrow. "Indeed I have."

"You didn't sell any of the jewellery yet?" asked Jess.

Mr Steen carefully brushed a speck of dust off the sleeve of his black suit. "Did the young lady change her mind? I rather thought she might." He motioned for Jess to follow him into the State Room. A black wooden box decorated with silver flowers lay on the table inside.

Jess picked up the ebony box. "Thank you! Everyone will be so pleased."

"Then you should take it to them straight away," Mr Steen told her. "And after that, remember that there are dishes to wash in the kitchen."

Jess dashed back upstairs. If only the gold silk dress had been as easy to find as this jewellery box. At least Alice wouldn't be in so much trouble now. Jess frowned. Why *had* Alice wanted to sell all her jewellery? It seemed a strange sort of thing to do.

Jess slowed down and took a peek in the box. There was a small pearl bracelet, a necklace with a diamond pendant shaped like a heart, a bracelet with rubies, three more necklaces and a cluster of rings. Altogether they would have earned Alice a lot of money.

"Oh, you found it!" Millie appeared at the corner of the gallery.

"Mr Steen had put it safely in the State

Room," said Jess. "I think he expected Alice to change her mind. Why did she want to sell her things anyway?"

"She hasn't explained yet," said Millie. "Lady Havering started wobbling as if she was going to faint and my mother was fanning her. Then, as the rain's stopped, we took my aunt to the courtyard for some fresh air."

Together the girls went down the grand staircase and through the parlour. Queen Belinda, Lady Havering, Veronica and Alice were sitting in the pretty courtyard. The queen was wafting Lady Havering with a peach coloured fan. Veronica wore a sulky look while Alice was staring at her hands which were folded tightly in her lap.

Millie opened the courtyard door, saying cheerfully, "It's all right! Jess asked Mr Steen for the jewellery box and here it is."

Jess set the box down on the table. Lady Havering snatched it up and began counting the things inside. Alice's cheeks grew pink. Jess stared at the girl curiously. Surely Alice didn't need money so much that she had to sell her things?

"Ahem!" Mr Steen appeared behind Jess and gave a polite cough. "Your Majesty." He bowed to the queen. "If you don't mind, I have a visitor for Jess."

Jess looked round in surprise. There was a boy standing in the doorway with a grey stripy cap in his hand. "Alfie!" She hurried over, drawing him into the parlour. "What are you doing here?"

"Hello, Jess! I came to deliver a letter. I thought while I was here I'd say hello—" Alfie broke off, staring. "Who's that girl with the dark hair?"

Jess followed his gaze. "That's Alice – why?"

"I've been trying to remember the person I saw in Buttons and Bows," Alfie told her. "Till now it was like a foggy picture in my head – just a person holding a dress in front of the mirror."

Jess's eyes widened. "And now you remember?"

"Clear as anything!" Alfie jerked his head towards the courtyard. "It was that girl with the dark hair. She's the one I saw!"

Chapter Ten
The Girl in Front of the Mirror

Jess's mouth dropped open. "You saw Alice by herself in Buttons and Bows? Are you sure?"

Alfie nodded. "The sun was shining and I could see right inside the shop. Now I've seen her again I know she was the girl in front of the mirror."

Jess's head was spinning. Could Alice have taken the dress? It didn't seem possible. She beckoned to Millie, who came hurrying in from the courtyard. Alfie did an awkward bow.

"Millie, this is Alfie who I told you about. You'll never guess who he saw yesterday in Buttons and Bows?" cried Jess.

"Who?" Millie said eagerly.

"Alice! She was there around the time the silk dress went missing." Jess glanced through the parlour window at Alice, who was still staring at her lap.

"Really!" Millie's eyes went round. "Does that mean she took it? I can't believe she would."

"I reckon you should ask her." Alfie put his cap on. "Now I'd better get on with my next delivery. Good day to you!"

Jess and Millie showed Alfie to the door and waved as he trudged back to the palace gate.

"Alfie's right!" said Jess. "We have to ask Alice what's going on."

"I still can't believe she would take something!" said Millie.

"How could she have managed it?" Jess frowned. "I was with her the whole time – first at the bakery and then at Miss Clackton's Pet Emporium."

Closing the palace door, they rushed back to the courtyard. The only person there was Veronica. "Where is everybody?" Millie asked the older girl.

Veronica took a spoonful of cream cake before answering. "Our mothers went to the rose garden. I don't know where Alice is. She started sulking when I told her that her freckles looked like breadcrumbs."

"Don't you think she might be upset?" said Millie.

"Oh, she's fine!" Veronica scooped up more cream. "You don't understand because you don't have a sister."

Jess rolled her eyes. "Let's try upstairs," she said to Millie. "Alice could be in her chamber."

They hurried upstairs but when they reached Alice's bedchamber they found it empty.

"Isn't Veronica awful? I feel sorry for Alice sometimes." Millie opened the wardrobe. "Look – her cloak's gone! Maybe she's gone out somewhere."

The girls raced downstairs to the palace entrance and then stopped to catch their breath.

"You could look around the stables and the lake," said Jess, "while I search the rose garden and the croquet lawn."

"Meet you back here!" cried Millie.

Jess raced round the side of the palace. Reaching the rose garden, she nearly ran into Queen Belinda and Lady Havering. Luckily they were bending over to sniff some yellow roses and she ducked behind a hedge just in time.

There was no sign of Alice. Jess couldn't see her on the croquet lawn either. She hesitated, trying to decide where to look. There was a faint noise like a cat meowing. Jess turned round but couldn't see the creature. Maybe the poor thing was stuck somewhere.

Listening closely, Jess followed the sound to the edge of the palace maze. The noise stopped and then began again with a funny hiccup. Jess frowned. Maybe it wasn't a cat after all.

"Jess!" Millie ran across the grass. "I can't find Alice anywhere."

Jess put a finger to her lips, whispering. "I think someone's crying."

The noise broke off for a moment. Then it started up again, a little louder.

"They must be inside the maze," Millie whispered back.

The girls ran down a path between the tall hedge walls of the maze. They stopped each time the path branched out, trying to work out which direction took them closer to the noise. The sobbing grew higher and ended in a loud hiccup.

Millie and Jess dashed round a corner and found Alice huddled on a wooden bench clutching a soggy handkerchief.

"Alice!" cried Jess. "Are you all right?"

Alice sniffed. Her nose was red and a tear glistened on her cheek. "I've done something horrible. Oh dear! I'll never be able to make it right."

Jess sat down on one side of her and Millie sat on the other. Alice wiped her face with her lacy handkerchief.

"Alice," began Millie. "Did you take the gold silk dress that was meant to be Veronica's?"

Alice started and her face went white. "How did you know?"

"A delivery boy saw you standing in front of the mirror with the dress," explained Millie. "But why did you do it?"

Alice began crying again and Millie patted her shoulder. Jess sighed. Half of her didn't like

to see Alice so upset, the other half felt cross about how much worry the girl had caused them all.

"I didn't mean to!" Alice said at last, mopping her cheeks again. "I just wanted to try the dress on. But when I held it up and looked in the mirror, I remembered all the things that Veronica had said. How it wouldn't suit me anyway and how I had too many freckles. I felt so cross and that's when I took it."

"But how did you manage it?" asked Millie. "Mr Heddon told us he didn't see anybody going into the shop. It's as if you were invisible!"

A sudden thought struck Jess. "Unless . . . I bet you didn't go through the front door at all!" She jumped up and started pacing across the grass. "We were together in the Pet Emporium when the parrot escaped. He flew all around the place and we chased him. You went to shut the back door so that he didn't fly away."

"That's right!" Alice sniffed. "I looked outside and that's when I realized I was right next to the yard behind Buttons and Bows."

Millie's eyes widened. "And then you slipped through the back gate between the two yards, didn't you? That's why no one saw you go inside the shop – you went through the back door!"

"I just wanted to look at the dress again," said Alice. "But there was no one else there and that's when I got the terrible thought that I could take the gold silk. Then Veronica wouldn't have it and that would serve her right for being so mean!" She broke into another torrent of tears.

Jess folded her arms. "I know Veronica

should have been nicer. But taking the dress was still wrong! My mother's been so worried and if it isn't found she'll have to pay all that money back."

"I'm sorry, Jess!" Alice's chin wobbled. "I never thought it would cause so much trouble for your parents. I'll pay the money back myself. That's why I was going to sell all my jewellery."

"Oh, that's why!" said Millie. "But honestly! Doesn't it make more sense just to put the dress back?"

"I can't!" wailed Alice. "I hid it in the storeroom of the Pet Emporium and piled lots of things on top of it. I'd never find it again!"

Millie bit her lip. "If we explained I'm sure Miss Clackton would let us search her storeroom. It could take a long time though."

"Not if we have a helper!" Jess's eyes sparkled. "We just need a creature that's brilliant at sniffing things out. I think we should take Jax with us!"

Chapter Eleven
The Best Dog in the World

"Good idea, Jess!" said Millie. "Jax is great at finding things. Remember how he discovered my glove in the stable yard that time? I bet he'll find the dress much quicker than us."

"We just need one of Veronica's garments to help him catch the right scent," said Jess. "Could you get that for us, Alice?"

"Of course!" Alice blinked away her tears.

"But aren't you going to tell my mother what I've done?"

Millie and Jess looked at each other. "Let's find the gold silk," said Jess. "Then I think *you* should decide who to tell."

"Thanks, Jess," Alice managed a smile. "You're very kind."

"Come on!" Millie pulled Alice to her feet. "We need to get to Bodkin Street."

Millie decided that the trip into Plumchester didn't need to be a secret. They could easily explain it to their mothers as a trip to Buttons and Bows. When they got back inside she asked the queen if they could go shopping. Then she told Mr Steen to send for a carriage.

Alice ran upstairs and reappeared with a silky white stocking that had turned a bit brown round the heel and toes.

Mr Steen's eyebrows rose at the sight of

the stocking dangling from Alice's fingers. "Shall I tell the coachman you're ready, Princess Amelia?"

"Er, yes! Thank you, Mr Steen." Millie climbed into the carriage followed by Alice. "We're just waiting for Jess."

"Here I am!" Jess ran down the front steps pulling Jax on his lead. The spaniel's golden tail wagged joyfully as he sprang into the carriage.

The coachman called to the horses and the carriage rolled forward. Alice fell silent and twisted the stocking in her lap. "What if we can't find the dress?" she said at last.

"We have to find it," said Jess firmly.

"You'll help us, won't you, Jax?" Millie rubbed the dog's soft fur.

The carriage stopped in Bodkin Street and the girls hurried into Miss Clackton's Pet Emporium. The kittens in their basket beside the counter stared at Jax with big dark eyes. Henry the parrot squawked loudly.

"Good morning!" Miss Clackton came bustling out of the back room. "Thank you, Henry! He's better than having a doorbell – always lets me know when there's a customer. Now what can I do for you? Something nice for this lovely dog? A treat maybe?"

Jax barked at the word "treat".

Millie glanced at Alice, who'd turned as red as the parrot's tail feathers. "Actually, we're looking for something. Alice says she left something in your storeroom yesterday."

"Bless me! Are you sure?" Miss Clackton pushed on her glasses and peered at Alice.

"It was when Henry escaped and flew all over the place," explained Jess.

"I'm really sorry to cause trouble, Miss Clackton," faltered Alice. "Please may I look for it?"

"Of course you can! I'd love to help but I must give the kittens their milk." Miss Clackton beamed at Alice, adding to herself. "Such a lovely polite girl."

Alice reddened even further. The three girls crowded into the storeroom where the shelves were crammed with tins and boxes.

"I've had a tidy up in there and moved things around," Miss Clackton called after them. "I hope that doesn't make it trickier."

Millie gazed at the towering piles of cat treats and doggie beds. "Do you remember where you put it?" she asked Alice.

"I think it was there." Alice pointed at the left hand corner. "Right behind that empty birdcage."

Millie climbed up on a box and peered

into the dark space. There was no gleam of gold material. She lifted down the birdcage but there was nothing behind it at all. "You have a look, Alice."

Climbing on to the box, Alice stared into the corner. "I can't see it. I'm not even sure this was where I put it after all."

"Pass me Veronica's stocking." Jess took the long white sock and knelt down beside the golden spaniel. "Here you are, Jax. This is the scent we need you to find." She let him sniff the stocking for a little while before putting the garment in her apron pocket.

Jax lifted his nose in the air. Then he circled the store room three times, sniffing boxes and tins.

Millie held her breath. In a room so full of stuff, Jax was their best chance of finding the silk. She hoped his sense of smell was good enough. She glanced at Alice, who was clasping her hands tightly. If only her cousin had owned up to taking the dress straight away. They could have sorted this out much sooner.

Jax stopped circling the storeroom and pawed at a wooden crate.

Jess swooped down. "Have you found it? Well done, boy!" She lifted the crate's lid to find a pile of dog bowls made from blue china. "Oh!" Her face fell.

Millie delved into the box but there was nothing else there. "What was it, Jax?"

Jax gave a long whine and pawed the box again.

"Maybe the dress is stuck behind it," said Millie. "Quick, help me pull it out!"

The girls grabbed the corners of the box and pulled together. The china bowls rattled as the crate slid slowly across the floor. Jax barked and wagged his tail.

"Can you see anything, Millie?" asked Jess.

"I don't think so." Millie peered round the crate. A patch of gold gleamed right at the back. "Wait! I think I do see something." She reached round the box and her fingertips brushed against smooth silk.

Millie's heart skipped as she pulled the cloth gently. Little by little, she drew out the gold silk and brushed off the dust. "It's a bit smudged but it's definitely Veronica's dress," she beamed. "We found it!"

"I didn't put it there," said Alice. "It must have fallen down the gap at the back of the shelf. Thank you so much for finding it."

"You should thank Jax really," said Jess. "He did all the hard work!"

Alice knelt down to hug the golden spaniel. She rested her cheek against his soft coat. "Thanks, Jax. You're the best dog in the world."

Millie smoothed the creases out of the

silk. “Shall we go to Buttons and Bows?”

Jess nodded. “Mother will be so happy when we tell her we’ve found it!”

Chapter Twelve
Making Amends

Jess burst through the door of Buttons and Bows, making the bell jingle wildly. Alice followed her and Millie came in last, holding on to Jax's lead. Jess's parents were talking quietly by the counter.

Jess looked round, surprised to see the shop so empty. "Mother! Father! Where is everyone?"

Her mother smiled faintly. Her face was pale. "Hello, Jess! We didn't know you'd visit this morning. I'm afraid we haven't had many customers so far."

"People may have heard about the missing silk." Jess's father rubbed his beard. "I hope they aren't keeping away because of it."

"They won't need to!" Jess took the silk dress from Millie and gave it to her mother. "We found this! Now everything will be all right again!"

"I don't believe it!" Mrs Woolhead gasped. "That's wonderful! I'd given up hope of getting it back." She held up the garment. The gold silk shimmered in the sunlight pouring through the shop window.

"Well done, girls!" said Mr Woolhead. "But how on earth did you find it?"

Jess bit her lip. She'd promised Alice in the maze that telling her secret was her choice. At the same time, Jess didn't like keeping things from her mother and father.

"We knew where the dress might be," she began.

"And Jax helped us a lot with his amazing sense of smell." Millie patted Jax's coat.

"It's all my fault!" Alice burst out. "I'm really sorry!" She rubbed her eyes and took a huge gulping breath.

"Oh dear!" Mrs Woolhead put her arm round Alice. "Please don't get upset. I'm sure it wasn't really your fault."

"It was!" cried Alice. "I took the dress because I was cross with Veronica. She always gets the nicest things and she pretends it's because she's the best. But I never thought it would cause you all this worry. I wish I'd never done it!"

Mr Woolhead looked thoughtful. "It has been a lot of trouble but you did the right thing in the end. Isn't that so, Jess?"

Jess looked at Alice's tear-stained face

and suddenly she knew she had to forgive her. She smiled. "I think everyone makes mistakes sometimes. You just have to make sure you put them right."

"I will!" nodded Alice. "I can make up for my mistake. I'll wash all the smudges off Veronica's dress so that it's perfect again. Then I'll sweep – if you show me how to do it – and I'll even scrub the floor!"

Mr and Mrs Woolhead agreed that Alice could help out for a while. Mr Woolhead left to collect some cloth from the market. Alice began washing the gold silk dress while Jess and Millie got lunch ready. Mrs Woolhead took Jax into the back yard where he fell asleep in the sun.

Alice bent her dark head over the basin of soapy water. She rubbed the gold silk gently. When the smudges faded, she rinsed the dress with clean water and hung it outside to dry. Then she asked Jess to show her how to sweep.

"That's really good." Jess watched approvingly as Alice swung the broom quickly across the floor.

"It's quite fun!" Alice smiled. "My arms are tired though."

"The floor looks great," said Jess. "Let's have some lunch."

They sat on the bench in the back yard to eat bread rolls and little apricot pies. Then Mrs Woolhead offered them a slice of her ginger loaf. After lunch, Alice mopped the floor, cleaned the windows and put together a new window display using brightly coloured scarves and bonnets.

"There! I've finished these." Mrs Woolhead held up two dresses. Alice's orange satin was now stitched together neatly with silver buttons down the back and small satin

roses at the waist. Veronica's gold dress had sparkling diamond beads sewn all across the top.

"I love the little roses you've put on

my dress," said Alice. "Thank you, Mrs Woolhead."

"Shall we take the dresses back to the palace for Lady Havering?" asked Jess.

Mrs Woolhead smiled. "Let me just wrap them up nicely in paper."

Lady Havering pounced on Jess, Millie and Alice as soon as they entered the palace. "Girls, what has taken you so long and why are you so dusty?"

"We went to collect Alice's dress from Buttons and Bows," explained Millie. "We found Veronica's dress too!"

Jess unwrapped the parcel with the dresses. Lady Havering snatched up the gold silk and studied it suspiciously. A smile broke out on her sharp face. "That looks wonderful with the added diamond beads. Well, Bess! Your mother certainly is an excellent dressmaker. Please send her my good wishes."

"I will." Jess tried not to giggle at being called the wrong name.

"Veronica!" Lady Havering called up the stairs. Then she saw Mr Steen hovering nearby. "Fetch my eldest daughter, would you please?"

Veronica came down a minute later and her eyes lit up when she saw her dress. "Can I try it on, Mother?" She held the dress against her. "I'm going to look fabulous – much better than Alice in her orange thing!"

"Veronica! That is *not* polite." Lady Havering took the gold dress back. "Return to your room at once and think about your manners."

Veronica opened her mouth to argue but Lady Havering gave her a stern look.

Flushing, Veronica marched out of the room.

"I'll try mine on, shall I, Mother?" asked Alice and her mother nodded.

"I think you'll look lovely," Millie told Alice. "The dress looks more peach coloured than orange. Doesn't it, Jess?"

Jess smiled. "It does! You could wear your pearl bracelet with it too."

That evening after tea, Jess and Millie took Jax outside for a run.

"He needs a treat after what he's done today," said Millie, watching the spaniel bounding down the hill.

"Let's throw a stick in the lake for him," said Jess, grinning. "There's nothing he likes better than that!" She snapped a piece off a fallen branch and tossed it into the water.

With a joyful bark, Jax leapt into the lake splashing water everywhere.

"I'm glad we worked out the secret of the silk dress," said Millie. "And everything turned out all right in the end."

"I think Alice learned her lesson," said Jess.

"And we're getting very good at untangling secrets," added Millie. "Maybe it could be our job: Millie and Jess, the mystery-solving Double Trouble!"

"Then I hope the next puzzle is something really spooky," Jess's eyes sparkled, "like a ghost in the banquet hall or creepy sounds coming from the maze at midnight!"

Millie grinned. "Maybe Mr Larum's books will disappear and I'll have to miss a whole week of mathematics!"

The setting sun cast an orange glow across Peveril Palace. Jax bounded out of the water with his stick and followed the girls. Millie and Jess crossed the wooden bridge that spanned the lake, dreaming of new adventures.

Turn over for some fun puzzles and quizzes – grab a friend and play together!

Find the characters

Can you find the nine characters from the book within the word search?

T	P	G	M	H	J	A	X	F	M
M	B	A	R	G	E	A	N	K	R
R	I	U	B	N	A	D	J	P	L
S	A	M	I	L	L	I	E	W	A
T	Q	M	B	T	I	U	S	H	R
E	D	X	B	B	C	I	S	D	U
E	S	I	Y	W	E	F	J	G	M
N	U	K	D	A	L	F	I	E	R
A	T	N	H	B	S	T	V	R	E
Z	V	E	R	O	N	I	C	A	L

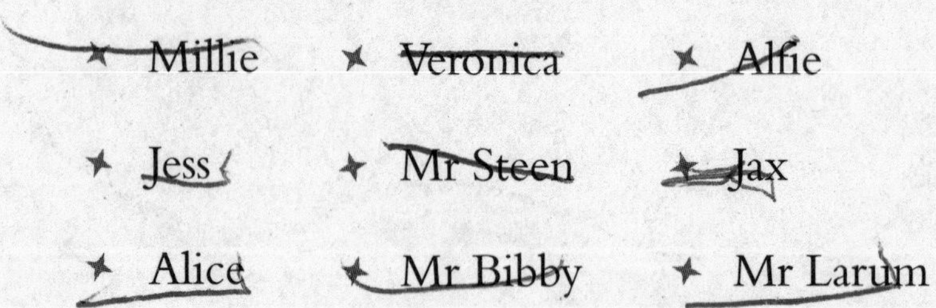

Let's get creative!

Design your own royal gown...

Ice Pops!

Make your own strawberry and banana ice pops. Remember, you must have an adult around to help you whizz the ingredients together!

Ingredients

- 120ml yoghurt
- 60ml milk
- 10 strawberries
- 1 ripe banana
- 1-2 tablespoons of honey

Equipment

Ice lolly mould

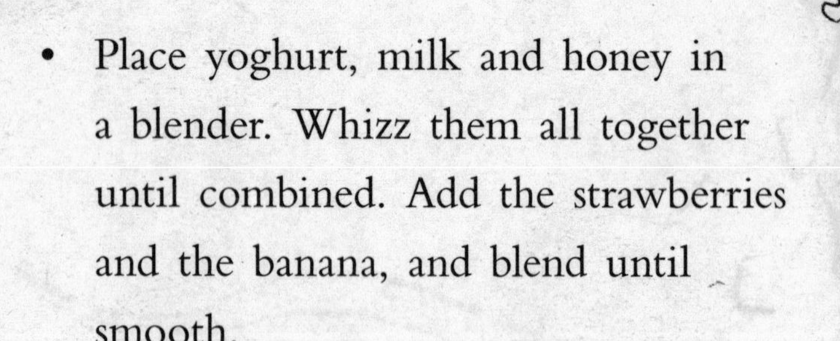

- Place yoghurt, milk and honey in a blender. Whizz them all together until combined. Add the strawberries and the banana, and blend until smooth.

- Carefully pour the mixture into the ice lolly moulds and pop in the freezer for at least 5-6 hours. (Ask your adult to help you if it's too difficult)!

Top Tip...

Once your ice lollies are frozen, try putting them in a container with some warm water so they can easily slide out of their moulds.

Spot the Difference

Can you spot the five differences?

Find that dress!

Can you lead Millie and Jess
to the silk dress?

Who could it be?

Connect the dots to reveal which creature is hiding amidst the dots...

Turn the page for a peek at another Tiara Friends adventure...

Chapter One
Cake Mixture

Millie stirred the cake mixture so fast that the spoon flew round the bowl. She had to make sure there were no lumps. The cake was for her brother Prince Edward's first birthday and she wanted it to be perfect. Her arm started to ache but she kept on stirring.

The mixture turned beautifully smooth and golden. A curl escaped from Millie's white mob cap and a spot of mixture splattered on to her maid's apron. A cheerful fire warmed the palace kitchen. Gleaming saucepans hung on the wall and there were shelves filled with pots of herbs and spices.

"Can I lick the spoon yet?" Jess danced round the table, her green satin dress swishing as she twirled. Hop – step, step, spin. Her hair, tied up with a green velvet ribbon, bounced as she moved.

Millie smiled at her friend. "Soon! It's nearly done."

A plump woman with grey hair bustled out of the pantry. "There! That's all the deliveries put away." She wiped her hands on her apron and peered at the mixing bowl. "How are you getting on with that mixture, Jess? Did you see the practice cake I made yesterday?" She pointed to a finished cake. "Looks like your fresh one will be even nicer."

The two girls exchanged looks.

"Yes, I think it's nearly ready." Millie smiled at Cook. "But actually, I'm not Jess. I'm Millie!"

Cook Walsh laughed and shook her head. "Goodness me! Of course it's you, Princess Amelia! You girls are such scamps for swapping places.

Mind you don't get caught!" She took the mixing bowl from Millie and gave it an extra stir.

"No one ever notices!" said Jess, twirling again. "I've just been to Millie's ballroom-dancing lesson and Miss Parnell didn't suspect a thing."

Amelia (Millie for short) and Jess had been best friends ever since Jess became a maid at Peveril Palace three years ago. Jess's parents owned a dressmaking shop a few streets away. Jess's mother had made clothes for Millie since she was little and was well-respected at the palace. Jess had a chamber near the kitchen where she stayed most of the week, going home to stay with her parents on her days off.

The two girls were born in the same month; although Millie was fond of pointing out that she was ten days older. They both had glossy brown hair with hints of gold at the front. Their eyes were hazel, though Jess's were a little darker. They were exactly the same height. In fact they were so similar that it was very hard to tell them apart.

Queen Belinda and Mary, Jess's mother, had thought the likeness very handy. It meant Jess could do dress fittings for the princess's clothes while Millie was busy with other royal duties. But as soon as Jess tried on Millie's things, Millie wanted to try on Jess's. Since then, the two girls had swapped clothes more times than they could count and all without anyone (except Cook) finding out their secret.

Cook shook her head again. "Well, just be careful! Goodness knows what the queen would say if she saw you in that cap and apron. Now let's get this practice cake out of the way and put your fresh one in the oven." She lifted the finished cake off the table and put it on the side.

"I like wearing Jess's uniform." Millie smoothed the white apron. "Especially if it means I get a chance to bake a cake!"

"And I like taking dance lessons." Jess did a pirouette. "Though I don't think I'd want to wear this dress ALL day long."

Cook Walsh smiled at them affectionately. "Who would have thought it? Peveril Palace has a maid that likes ballroom dancing and a princess that loves baking. The world is a funny place!"

The girls smiled back, their cheeks dimpling in exactly the same place and their hazel eyes sparkling.

"It's true!" said Jess. "We may look the same but we don't like the same things at all! C'mon, Millie. If you've finished cooking I'd better teach you the new dance steps I learned. You'll need to know them for the party."

There were footsteps in the passageway.

"Cook Walsh, have you seen Princess Amelia?" called Queen Belinda. "I've been looking for her everywhere!"

Millie jumped and her mob cap fell off. She grabbed it and quickly crammed it back on her head. "Jess, what shall we do?" she whispered.

"You have to act like you're me," hissed Jess. "I'll hide!" She dashed into the pantry and closed the door behind her.

The queen walked into the kitchen carrying Prince Edward. The little prince waved his chubby arms and gurgled. He was dressed in velvet breeches and a frilly white shirt. On top of his blond curls was a little golden crown sparkling with diamonds.

"Good morning, Your Majesty," said

Cook. "Oh, look at the little prince! How gorgeous he looks in his crown."

Millie, who had busied herself tidying the table when her mother came in, risked a quick look over her shoulder. Her baby brother did look quite sweet. She recognized the golden circlet on Edward's head. It was called the Baby Diamond Crown. It had been worn by each royal baby on their first birthday for hundreds of years.

Queen Belinda smiled. "Thank you, Cook! I wanted to put his party clothes on to make sure they fit. All the guests will want to see him looking smart and wearing the Baby Diamond Crown. It's traditional!" The queen gently stopped the baby prince from grabbing the crown and pulling it off. "If you see Amelia could you tell her I need her upstairs straight away," she continued. "I want her to try on her party clothes too. I think the dress may need some lace and beads to finish it off."

"I'll tell her, Your Majesty," replied Cook Walsh.

Millie pulled her cap lower as the queen swept past. Cook was right. Her mother would have quite a few things to say if she found out that Millie and Jess had swapped places. Queen Belinda could be quite strict about royal rules and etiquette.

The pantry door opened a little and Jess peered round. "Is it safe?"

"She's gone! We'd better go and swap clothes again." Millie gave Cook a quick hug. "Thanks, Cook! I loved helping with the cake."

Cook smiled. "Off you go now! And remember: your mother wants you straight away."

Millie and Jess ran up the bare wooden stairs to Millie's royal chamber. Millie wasn't really supposed to use the back stairs as they were for the servants, but it was quicker, and the brass stair rail on the first floor was brilliant for sliding down.

There was no time for sliding this morning.

Jess and Millie took the left passageway leading to the royal chambers. Lanterns fixed to the wall cast a dim light over the corridor. Kings and queens with stern eyes stared down from dark paintings. Millie tried not to look at them too much. She started imagining they didn't approve of her wearing a maid's uniform. *Don't be silly*, she told herself, *they're just pictures!*

Another maid called Connie came out of a nearby chamber carrying a tray of cups and plates. She hardly glanced at the girls. Connie was three years older and thought she was ever so grown-up!

As Connie passed, there was a sharp click at the far end of the passage. A shadowy figure closed the door to the queen's chamber and ran away. In the gloom Millie couldn't make out who it was. The figure vanished round the corner into the long gallery.

"Was that Mr Steen?" whispered Jess. "I couldn't see."

Millie frowned. "I don't know." There

was something strange about the way the person had scuttled away. Mr Steen was the royal butler and liked to roam the palace giving out orders, but he didn't usually run around like that.

"If it was him we should get out of here before he comes back," urged Jess. "He's bound to have a long list of jobs he wants me do to." She eyed Millie in the maid uniform. "Actually he'll just give all the scrubbing and dusting to you!"

"That sounds even worse than Miss Parnell's dancing lessons!" Millie pulled a funny look of horror. "C'mon!" Grabbing Jess's hand, she dragged her along the corridor.

The girls dashed into Millie's chamber, quickly shut the door and fell on the bed giggling.